This book belongs to :

Sir Garibald and Hot Nose

First published in Great Britain in 1996 by
Macdonald Young Books

加里波爵士與噴火龍哈諾

Marjorie Newman 著
Christopher Masters 繪
刊欣媒體營造工作室 譯

三民書局

Chapter One

Sir Garibald lived with his dragon Hot Nose in a dark, **creepy castle** in the mountains.

The castle was especially dark and creepy at night. Then it was **lit** only by candles and Hot Nose's fiery breath. Sir Garibald and Hot Nose kept nearly **jumping out of their skins** with fright.

Even so, they never thought of changing things. Until...

第一章

加里波爵士和他的噴火龍哈諾住在山上一座黑漆漆、陰森森的城堡裡。

一到晚上，城堡就更黑暗、更可怕了，只能藉著蠟燭和哈諾吐出的火焰來照明。加里波爵士和哈諾因為害怕只好不停地跳來跳去。

即使如此，他們卻從未想過要做任何改變，直到……

creepy [`kripɪ] 形 令人毛骨悚然的
castle [`kæsl̩] 名 城堡
light [laɪt] 動 照亮（過去分詞 lit [lɪt]）
jump out of one's skin
（高興、緊張得）不能自制地跳起來

One day Sir Garibald was asked to visit the nearest school and tell the children about **knights** in the old days.

He told them about castles, and **rescuing** people, and fighting dragons. Afterwards the children showed him one of their school **video games**. It was about a knight.

Sir Garibald loved the video game. The children showed him some more. Sir Garibald was still playing the games at home time.

有一天，最近的一所學校邀請加里波爵士到學校為小朋友講述古代騎士的種種。

他告訴小朋友關於城堡、解救百姓、還有對抗龍的故事；然後小朋友向他展示學校的電腦益智遊戲——那是一個以騎士為主題的遊戲。

加里波爵士很喜歡這個電腦益智遊戲，小朋友還展示了其他的遊戲給他看。加里波爵士一直玩到放學時間還意猶未盡。

knight [naɪt] 名 騎士
rescue [`rɛskjʊ] 動 解救
video game 電動玩具

It was quite late before he **hurried** back up the mountain to his dark, creepy castle.

"Hot Nose!" he **yelled**, **stumbling** over the front doorstep because he couldn't see it properly (*and* because he had very big feet). "Hot Nose! Where are you? We've got to get some video games!"

Hot Nose had hidden under the kitchen table when he heard all the shouting. Now he came out. He lit ten candles at once with his fiery breath.

等到加里波爵士趕忙上山，回到他那黑漆漆、陰森森的城堡時，時間已經很晚了。

「哈諾！」他大聲地叫著，因為看不清楚路（而且因為他有一雙很大的腳）而被前門的臺階絆倒了。「哈諾！你在哪裡？我們去弄些電腦益智遊戲來玩！」

哈諾本來躲在廚房的桌子底下，聽到加里波爵士的叫聲，便爬了出來，立刻從嘴巴吐出火焰點亮十根蠟燭。

hurry [ˋhɝɪ] 動 急忙
yell [jɛl] 動 喊叫
stumble [ˋstʌmbl̩] 動 絆倒 《over》

"Video games?" he asked. "Played on computers?"

"Yes! Yes!" cried Sir Garibald.

"Then we'll need **electricity**," said Hot Nose. "This castle hasn't *got* electricity."

"Oh," said Sir Garibald. With a **sinking** feeling he realized Hot Nose was right. "Never mind!" he cried. "We shall have electricity! I'll get it **put in**!"

"Electric lights, and hot water, and all that sort of thing?" asked Hot Nose.

"All that sort of thing!" **promised** Sir Garibald.

「電腦益智遊戲？」哈諾問，「是在電腦上玩的那一種嗎？」

「對啊！對啊！」加里波爵士大聲回答。

「那麼我們得要有『電』才行，」哈諾說，「我們的城堡裡並沒有電啊！」

「喔！」加里波爵士覺得很沮喪，因為哈諾說的一點兒也沒錯。「沒關係！」他大叫，「我們會有電，我來申請。」

「那就會有電燈、熱水、還有其他需要用『電』的東西囉？」哈諾問。

「沒錯！」加里波爵士保證著。

electricity [ɪ͵lɛk`trɪsətɪ] 名 電
sinking [`sɪŋkɪŋ] 形 沮喪的
put in 申請
promise [`pramɪs] 動 允諾，保證

"And the castle won't be creepy any more?" asked Hot Nose.

"Not a bit creepy," promised Sir Garibald.

"**Hooray**!" shouted Hot Nose. "How much will it cost?"

"Ah," said Sir Garibald. "Quite a lot, I expect. **Fetch** your **savings**, Hot Nose!"

Quietly, Hot Nose fetched his savings from his secret hiding place.

「然後城堡就不再陰森森了？」哈諾問。

「一點兒也不會了。」加里波爵士保證著。

「萬歲！」哈諾高興地叫著。「那要花多少錢啊？」

「嗯！」加里波爵士說，「我想會花很多錢。把你存的錢拿來，哈諾！」

哈諾安安靜靜地去他祕密藏錢的地方把錢拿出來。

hooray [hʊˋre] 感 萬歲
(= hurrah [həˋrɔ])
fetch [fɛtʃ] 動 把…拿來
savings [ˋsevɪŋz] 名 存款

Noisily, **bumping** about in the darkness — and **tripping** over his big feet quite a lot — Sir Garibald fetched *his* savings from his secret hiding place.

They **tipped** the money onto the kitchen table, and looked at it in the candlelight.

It was a very small pile.

"I'm afraid that won't be enough," sighed Sir Garibald.

"I'm sure it won't be enough," agreed Hot Nose. "We'll have to get more."

加里波爵士在黑暗中乒乒砰砰地——還被自己的大腳絆倒，摔了一大跤——也從他祕密藏錢的地方把錢拿出來。

他們把錢倒在廚房的桌上，在蠟燭的微光下看著這一點點的錢。

「我想錢恐怕不夠吧！」加里波爵士嘆著氣說。

「一定不夠！」哈諾也同意，「我們需要想辦法弄到更多的錢。」

bump [bʌmp] 動 碰撞
trip [trɪp] 動 絆倒 《over》
tip [tɪp] 動 倒出

"How?" asked Sir Garibald.

Hot Nose thought for a moment. Then he smiled a **crafty** smile.

"In the old days," he **remarked**, "knights had the very bad habit of fighting dragons."

"Yes," agreed Sir Garibald, puzzled.

"And got a **reward**," said Hot Nose.

"Yes," agreed Sir Garibald.

"Well...." said Hot Nose. He **whispered** in Sir Garibald's ear.

Sir Garibald began to smile.

"But...is that quite... honest?" he asked. "And will it work?"

「要怎麼做呢？」加里波爵士問。

哈諾想了一會兒，然後露出一個狡詐的笑容。

「從前啊！」他說，「騎士們有一個很壞的習慣，喜歡對付龍。」

「是啊！」加里波爵士雖然認同哈諾說的話，卻被弄得一頭霧水。

「還會因此得到一筆獎金哦！」哈諾接著說。

「是沒錯！」加里波爵士贊同地應著。

「所以……」哈諾湊到加里波爵士的耳邊說了一些話。

加里波爵士露出了微笑。

「可是……那會不會有點兒……不誠實？」加里波爵士問，「不過會成功吧？」

crafty [`kræftɪ] 形 狡詐的
remark [rɪ`mark] 動 陳述
reward [rɪ`wɔrd] 名 賞金
whisper [`hwɪspɚ] 動 耳語

Chapter Two

Early next morning Hot Nose **flapped** quietly away from the castle. It was very cold, but he was too full of his plan to **notice**. He flew on until **presently**, down below, he saw the village of Nettleford. It was what he had been looking for. No one in Nettleford would know himself and Sir Garibald.

第二章

第二天一早，哈諾靜悄悄地飛出了城堡。天氣很冷，不過哈諾滿心想著他的計畫，並不覺得冷。飛了一會兒，哈諾往下一看，看到尼陀福特村，那正是他一直在尋找的地方。因為在尼陀福特村中，不會有人認識他和加里波爵士。

flap [flæp] 動 振翅飛走《away》
notice [ˋnotɪs] 動 注意
presently [ˋprɛzn̩tlɪ] 副 不久 (= soon)

He **zoomed** down onto the church roof.

The wind blew cold. Now and again a car drove along the narrow **winding** street to the village **square**. Aunty Flo stood in the phone box, talking to a friend who lived in the nearby village of Greenways. Everything was peaceful.

Hot Nose **grinned**. Then, suddenly, he stood up, flapped his wings, and took off. Round and round the village he flew, just above the roof tops. Every now and again he let out a **mighty** 'Whooooosh!' of fire.

哈諾降落在教堂的屋頂上。

冷風呼呼地吹著，偶爾會有輛車子沿著狹窄蜿蜒的街道駛向村中的廣場。芙洛阿姨正在電話亭裡打電話給住在附近格林威治村的朋友。一切看來都很祥和。

哈諾露出微笑。突然間，他站了起來，揮動著翅膀，飛向天空。他貼著屋頂上方、繞著村莊飛了一圈又一圈，還不時有力的「呼嘘！」一聲噴出烈火。

zoom [zum] 動 奔馳，呼嘯而過
winding [`waɪndɪŋ] 形 蜿蜒的
square [skwɛr] 名 廣場
grin [grɪn] 動 露齒而笑
mighty [`maɪtɪ] 形 強而有力的

Down below there was **uproar**. Drivers looked up, and their cars **crashed** into hedges or ditches. Babies cried. Cats meowed. Dogs yelped. Ducks quacked. Aunty Flo **screamed**.

The children in the village school **rushed** to look out of the windows.

"It's a dragon!" they cried.

Hot Nose had a **marvelous** time, **soaring** and whooshing and flapping his wings.

The policeman came running out. He **radioed** for the **fire brigade**. Then he called to Hot Nose on his **loudspeaker** to come down.

The firefighters arrived. They **aimed** their hoses at Hot Nose. But they couldn't aim them as fast as Hot Nose could **twist** and turn. The firefighters got in a terrible **mess**.

The children laughed so much they could hardly stand up.

下面起了一陣騷動。開車的人紛紛抬起頭來張望，車子因此撞向籬笆或掉進水溝，嬰兒哭喊著，貓咪喵喵地叫，狗兒汪汪地吠，鴨子呱呱不停，芙洛阿姨也大聲尖叫起來。

村裡的學童紛紛擠到窗邊湊熱鬧。

「是龍吔！」他們叫著。

哈諾一面振翅飛舞，一面吐出火焰，可真威風啊！

uproar [ˋʌp͵ror] 名 騷動
crash [kræʃ] 動 碰撞
scream [skrim] 動 尖叫
rush [rʌʃ] 動 衝，蜂湧而至
marvelous [ˋmɑrvḷəs] 形 好極了的
soar [sor] 動 翱翔

警察跑了出來，用無線電呼叫消防隊，然後用擴音器喊話叫哈諾下來。

消防隊員到達後，把水管對著哈諾噴水，但是因為哈諾不停扭動身體，消防隊員無法瞄準，弄得一團混亂。

孩童看得幾乎笑彎了腰。

radio [ˋredɪ,o] 動 用無線電通知
fire brigade 消防隊
loudspeaker [ˋlaʊdˋspikɚ] 名 擴音器
aim [em] 動 把…瞄準… 《at》
twist [twɪst] 動 扭轉身體
mess [mɛs] 名 麻煩的局勢

Hot Nose laughed so much he could hardly fly. Then he decided it was time for the rest of his plan, and zoomed off.

The policeman and the firefighters **mopped** their brows.

"It's gone," they said. "We've frightened it away. You don't have to worry any more." They helped to rescue the cars from ditches and the **quivering** cats from tree tops.

哈諾也笑得幾乎飛不下去。然後他決定進行下一步計畫，便疾速地飛離了村子。

警察和消防隊員擦了擦額頭。

「他走了，」他們說，「我們把他嚇跑了。大家不用再擔心了。」大家一起幫忙把車子從水溝裡拉上來，把嚇得發抖的貓從樹上救下來。

mop [mɑp] 動 擦去…的汗水

quiver [`kwɪvɚ] 動 顫抖

Then the policeman and the firefighters were called away to other **urgent** jobs.

"Thank goodness that's over," said the villagers. They went home to make themselves **strong** cups of tea.

But Hot Nose was only flying back to the dark, creepy castle in the mountains, thinking about Part Two of his plan....

然後警察和消防隊員又被呼叫去處理其他緊急事故了。

「感謝老天，一切都結束了。」村民說著，一邊回家為自己泡杯濃茶鎮靜一下。

而哈諾飛回山上那座黑漆漆、陰森森的城堡，一面思考著要如何進行第二步計畫……

He **landed** in the castle **courtyard**.

Sir Garibald rushed out, tripping over his big feet.

"What happened?" he cried.

"It all went **splendidly**!" said Hot Nose. "We're ready for Part Two!"

While Hot Nose got himself a quick (but large) **snack**, Sir Garibald got out his old **motorbike**.

他降落在城堡的院子裡。

加里波爵士連忙跑了出來，又被自己的大腳絆倒摔了一跤。

「怎麼樣了？」他問。

「一切進行得很順利呢！」哈諾說，「可以進行第二步了。」

哈諾飛快地享用一頓豐盛的點心，加里波爵士則騎上他那部老舊的摩托車出門去了。

land [lænd] 動 降落，著陸
courtyard [`kɔrt,jɑrd] 名 中庭
splendidly [`splɛndɪdlɪ] 副 令人滿意地
snack [snæk] 名 點心
motorbike [`motɚ,baɪk] 名 摩托車

It was hard to ride a motorbike wearing a suit of **armor** and carrying a **sword**. Sir Garibald fell off once or twice. Then he got his **balance**, and **spluttered** away toward Nettleford.

Presently Hot Nose took off again, flying after Sir Garibald.

要穿著全副盔甲、帶著寶劍騎摩托車可不容易。加里波爵士還因此跌倒一、二次，然後再爬起來，一面嘟囔著往尼陀福特村前去。

一會兒哈諾再度起飛，緊跟在加里波爵士身後。

armor [`ɑrmɚ] 名 盔甲
sword [sord] 名 劍
balance [`bæləns] 名 平衡
splutter [`splʌtɚ] 動 急急忙忙地說話；發出噼剝聲

Chapter Three

Hot Nose reached Nettleford first. He settled on the roof of the pub and let out a whoosh of fire.

Cats hissed, dogs barked, babies cried, ducks quacked, cars bumped, the children looked out of the school windows....

第三章

哈諾先抵達尼陀福特村。他停在酒吧的屋頂上並噴出一口火焰。

貓咪嘶嘶地叫、狗兒狂吠、嬰兒哭喊、鴨子呱呱不停、汽車相撞、孩童從學校的窗戶向外張望……

"It's back!" cried Aunty Flo. "Help! Help! Call the police and the fire brigade!"

But at that moment Sir Garibald's motorbike came spluttering down the village High Street. Sir Garibald **wobbled** to a stop. He **switched off** the engine.

"**I say**!" he called. "Is something wrong?"

"Wrong?" cried the villagers. "There's a dragon on the roof of the pub!"

「他回來了！」芙洛阿姨叫著，「救命啊！救命啊！快叫警察和消防隊啊！」

就在這個時候，加里波爵士騎著摩托車噗嗞噗嗞地沿著村中的大街過來。加里波爵士搖搖晃晃地停車，熄掉引擎。

「哎呀！發生了什麼事？」他大聲地說。

「什麼事？」村民叫著，「酒吧的屋頂上有一隻龍啊！」

wobble [ˋwabl̩] 動 搖晃蹣跚而行
switch [swɪtʃ] 動 開關
switch off　關掉（switch on　打開）
I say!　哎呀！嘿！

"Really?" said Sir Garibald. He looked up. Hot Nose let out another "whoosh" of fire.

"Aaaaaah!" screamed the villagers.

"Stop that, dragon!" **ordered** Sir Garibald.

Hot Nose let out another 'whoosh!', and flew down to sit across the roof of a car.

「真的嗎？」加里波爵士問著，抬起頭往上一看，哈諾正「呼嘘」地噴出另一道火焰。

「啊……！」村民尖叫著。

「龍啊！停下來！」加里波爵士命令著。

哈諾「呼嘘」一聲又噴出另一道火焰，並飛下來跨坐在一輛汽車的車頂上。

"Aaaaaah!" screamed the villagers again.

"Oooooooh!" cried the children, nearly **tumbling** out of the windows in excitement.

The **mayor** stepped forward.

"Something must be done," he said. "At once. Sir. I can see you are a knight. I know that knights fight dragons. They are better at fighting dragons than even the police or the fire brigade. If you will **get rid of** this dragon we will give you a big reward."

「啊……！」村民又尖叫起來。

「喔……！」孩童叫著，興奮地擠向窗口。

村長向前走了出來。

「我們必須立刻採取行動。」他說。「大人，看來您是一位騎士，我知道騎士會對付龍。跟警察或消防隊員比起來，騎士更善於與龍對抗。如果您能夠除去這隻龍，我們將會致贈您一大筆的獎金。」

tumble [ˋtʌmbl̩] 動 跌倒；滾落

mayor [ˋmeɚ] 名 村長，市長

get rid of... 除去…

Hot Nose almost grinned. Sir Garibald smiled.

"You'll give me some money?" he asked.

"Yes," promised the mayor.

"Very well," said Sir Garibald. "I will fight the dragon."

"Hooray!" shouted the people and most of the children.

"Don't hurt it!" cried the rest of the children. "Dragons are an **endangered species**!"

哈諾幾乎要笑出來了，加里波爵士也露出微笑。

「你們要給我錢？」他問。

「是的。」村長保證。

「很好，」加里波爵士說，「我來對付那隻龍。」

「萬歲！」大人和大多數的小孩歡呼起來。

其他的小孩則叫著：「不要傷害他呀！」「龍是瀕臨絕種的動物！」

endangered [ɪn`dendʒɚd] 形 瀕臨危險的
species [`spiʃɪz] 名（生物）種類
endangered species　瀕臨絕種的生物

Hot Nose almost said, "Too right!" Instead he let out a huge 'WHOOSH!' of fire and **slipped** down from the car roof. Slowly, **menacingly**, he made his way across the village square to where Sir Garibald stood.

"Aaaaah!" yelled the villagers, stepping backwards and falling over each other.

"Aaaaah!" yelled Sir Garibald, stepping backwards and falling over his big feet. Then he **remembered** it was only Hot Nose. He **scrambled** up again.

　　哈諾幾乎就要脫口說出「對極了！」，不過他趕緊「呼嘘」一聲噴出一大口火焰，並從車頂上滑下來。他慢慢地穿過村裡的廣場，向加里波爵士所站的地方逼近。

　　「啊！」村民邊尖叫邊往後退，跌成了一團。

　　「啊！」加里波爵士邊尖叫邊往後退，還被自己的大腳絆倒。然後他想起那只是哈諾，便爬了起來。

slip [slɪp] 動 滑
menacingly [`mɛnɪsɪŋlɪ] 副 脅迫地
remember [rɪ`mɛmbɚ] 動 想起
scramble [`skræmbl̩] 動 攀爬

"**On guard**!" he shouted. He pulled out his sword.

The fight was **terrific**, **except that** at no time did Sir Garibald touch Hot Nose, and at no time did Hot Nose touch Sir Garibald.

Backwards and forwards they went, **round and round**, with the villagers cheering and ooohing and aaahing, and the children hanging out of the school windows to see better.

「小心！」他大叫一聲，接著拔出了劍。

戰鬥進行得很激烈，只是加里波爵士一次也沒有碰觸到哈諾，而哈諾也沒有碰觸到加里波爵士。

在村民的加油、呼喊、尖叫聲中，他們來來回回地轉圈圈移動著，小朋友則攀在學校的窗戶上想要看得更清楚。

guard [gɑrd] 名 警戒
on guard　提高警覺
terrific [təˋrɪfɪk] 形 激烈的
except that...　除了…這一點，只是
round and round　兜圈子

After a while Hot Nose **pretended** to stumble. Sir Garibald rushed at him.

"Careful!" **muttered** Hot Nose. He **groaned**, **staggered**, and flew up into the sky. Flapping his wings loudly he **made off**.

He landed just out of sight on a small hill. Then he got out the **binoculars** he'd hidden earlier and **peeped** round some bushes. He could see the village square.

It was part of the plan. He had to watch what happened in case Sir Garibald needed him.

一會兒之後，哈諾假裝跌倒，加里波爵士抓住機會突襲。

「小心！」哈諾小聲地提醒。他呻吟了一聲、步履蹣跚，然後飛向天空，用力揮動翅膀逃走了。

哈諾降落在一處村民看不到的小山坡上，取出事先藏好的望遠鏡，躲在樹叢後偷看。從這兒他可以望見村裡的廣場。

這是計畫中的一部分，他必須觀察情況，看看加里波爵士是否需要他。

pretend [prɪ`tɛnd] 動 假裝
mutter [`mʌtɚ] 動 低聲說
groan [gron] 動 呻吟
stagger [`stægɚ] 動 跌跌撞撞
make off 急忙離開，逃走 (= make away)
binoculars [baɪ`nɑkjəlɚz] 名 雙筒望遠鏡
peep [pip] 動 偷看

Down in the square everyone cried, "Hooray! You've **saved** us, Sir Knight! You're so **brave**! Let's have a party!"

Sir Garibald was glad to sit down and get his breath back. Presently he joined in with the party. The mayor went off, and came back carrying a huge bag.

"The reward," he said.

He gave it to Sir Garibald.

At that very second some people from Greenways came rushing into the square.

廣場上所有的人都在歡呼，「萬歲！您救了我們，騎士大人，您好勇敢，我們開個派對慶祝慶祝吧！」

加里波爵士很高興能坐下來喘口氣，一會兒便加入了派對。村長走了出去，然後帶著一個大袋子回來。

「這是獎金。」他說。

村長把獎金交給加里波爵士。

就在這時，一些由格林威治村來的民眾衝進了廣場。

save [sev] 動 拯救
brave [brev] 形 勇敢的

"Where's the knight who fights dragons?" they cried. "We had a phone call about him from Aunty Flo!"

"Here he is!" cried the villagers, pushing Sir Garibald to the **front**.

"*We've* got a dragon!" cried the Greenways people. "It's been frightening us all day. It keeps **stamping** its feet, and breathing out fire! Please, Sir Knight, come and fight our dragon!"

「打敗龍的騎士在哪兒？」他們大喊著，「芙洛阿姨打電話告訴我們了！」

「他在這兒！」村民大聲回答，把加里波爵士推向前去。

「我們也有一隻龍！」格林威治的村民叫著，「那隻龍整天嚇唬我們，他不停地在跺腳、吐火焰！騎士大人，拜託您來幫我們對付那隻龍吧！」

front [frʌnt] 名 前面
stamp [stæmp] 動 用力跺腳

Sir Garibald **gulped**.

"Is it a f...f...**fierce**, wild dragon?" he **trembled**.

加里波爵士止住了呼吸。

「那……那……是……一隻兇猛的野龍嗎？」他用顫抖的聲音問著。

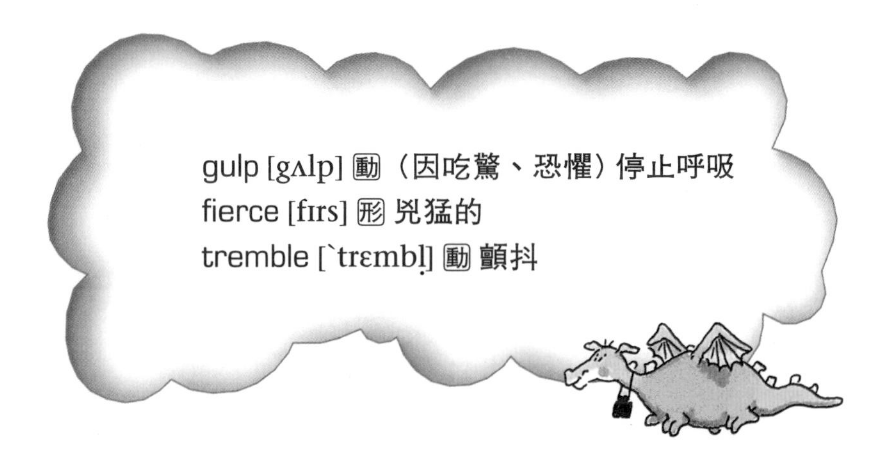

gulp [gʌlp] 動（因吃驚、恐懼）停止呼吸

fierce [fɪrs] 形 兇猛的

tremble [`trɛmbḷ] 動 顫抖

Chapter Four

"It looks like a *very* fierce, wild dragon!" said the people. "Please help us, before it eats us or sets fire to our houses!"

Sir Garibald tried to think. He didn't want to tell the villagers of Nettleford he'd been **tricking** them.

He *did* want to help the people from Greenways.

第四章

「看起來是一隻很兇猛的野龍哦！」村民說，「在他還沒吃掉我們或是燒了我們的房子之前，請您救救我們！」

加里波爵士考慮了一下。他不想告訴尼陀福特的村民說他欺騙了他們。

而他也真的想要幫助格林威治村的人。

trick [trɪk] 動 欺騙

But he did *not* want to fight a fierce, wild dragon.

"Um — I have to have a **rest** before I can answer," he said.

Hastily he got on his motorbike and spluttered off up the hill to find Hot Nose. Hot Nose saw him coming, and came out from the bushes.

"Ah!" yelled Sir Garibald.

"Oh. It's only you, Hot Nose. At first I thought it was another fierce, wild dragon."

不過他可不想對抗一隻兇猛的野龍。

「嗯——在答覆你們之前，我必須先休息一會兒。」他說。

他慌忙地騎上摩托車，噗嗞噗嗞地騎往小山坡去找哈諾。哈諾看見他來了，便從樹叢後走了出來。

「啊！」加里波爵士尖叫了一聲。

「喔！原來是你，哈諾。我還以為是另一隻兇猛的野龍呢！」

Quickly he told Hot Nose the story.

"No problem," said Hot Nose. "You must fight this other dragon. Then we'll have two rewards."

"No problem?" cried Sir Garibald. At that moment a dragon **roared**.

"Ah! He must be huge! We can hear him right up here!" cried Sir Garibald.

他很快地把經過情形告訴哈諾。

「沒問題。」哈諾說，「你必須對付那隻龍，這樣我們就會有二筆獎金了。」

「沒問題？」加里波爵士喊著。這時另一隻龍吼叫了起來。

「啊！他一定很龐大！我們在這小山上也聽得到他的聲音。」

He looked around. "Hot Nose?"

Hot Nose was hiding among the bushes. His voice was **muffled**. "I can see him. He's in Greenways' market place," he said. "You can easily fight him. I'll wait here!"

Sir Garibald had to **make up his mind**.

加里波爵士叫著，四處張望，「哈諾？」

哈諾躲到樹叢裡，壓低嗓音說：「我看見他了，他在格林威治村的市集裡。」他說，「你可以輕易打倒他的，我在這裡等你喲！」

加里波爵士必須做個決定了。

muffle [`mʌfl̩] 動 壓低⋯的聲音

make up one's mind 下定決心

Chapter Five

Slowly Sir Garibald rode back to the village. Slowly he got off his motorbike. Slowly he **handed** the reward money back to the mayor.

Hot Nose was watching. He couldn't **bear** it! Giving the money back?

The mayor and all the villagers were puzzled.

第五章

加里波爵士騎著摩托車慢慢地回到村裡，慢慢地熄掉引擎，慢慢地把獎金退還給村長。

哈諾看著這一切，實在感到無法忍受！他竟然把錢退回去？

村長和所有的村民都被弄糊塗了。

hand [hænd] 動 把…交給…
bear [bɛr] 動 忍受

"I'm sorry," said Sir Garibald. "I tricked you. The dragon I fought was my own dragon, Hot Nose. He's quite **harmless**. He's even just the **tiniest** bit **cowardly**.... We wanted some money so that we could have electricity put into our dark, creepy castle. Then we could play video games."

He stopped speaking.

Everyone was very quiet.

Then the people from Greenways said, "You mean ... you won't help us?"

「我很抱歉，」加里波爵士說，「我騙了你們，我所對付的那隻龍是我自己養的，叫做哈諾。他一點也不兇猛，甚至有點兒膽小……我們只是需要錢來為我們那座黑漆漆、又陰森森的城堡接上電力，然後我們就可以玩電腦益智遊戲。」

他沒有再說下去。

每個人都很安靜。

接著，格林威治的村民說：「您的意思是……您不幫助我們？」

harmless [`hɑrmlɪs] 形 無害的

tiny [`taɪnɪ] 形 極小的

cowardly [`kaʊɚdlɪ] 形 膽小的

They looked very **disappointed**.

Sir Garibald looked at them. After all, he *was* a knight. He **was supposed to** be brave. He was supposed to rescue people from dragons.

He took a deep breath.

"I'll try," he said.

"Hooray!" cried everyone.

The people from both villages **set out** down the road, with Sir Garibald wobbling slowly along on his motorbike. Presently the people stopped.

他們看來很失望。

加里波爵士看著他們。畢竟，他是一名騎士，他應該要勇敢，他應該要對付龍，解救百姓的。

他深吸了一口氣。

「我試試看。」他說。

「萬歲！」大夥兒歡呼起來。

加里波爵士在兩村村民的陪同下，搖搖晃晃地騎著摩托車慢慢前進。一會兒村民停了下來。

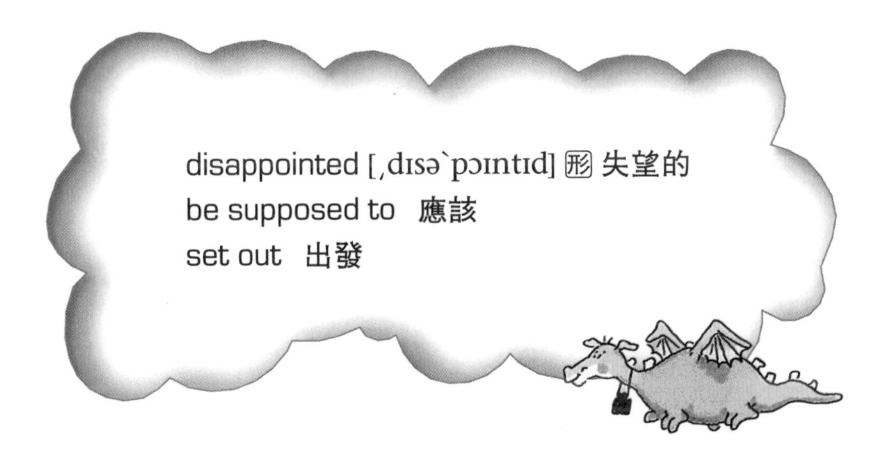

disappointed [ˌdɪsəˋpɔɪntɪd] 形 失望的

be supposed to　應該

set out　出發

"Just along there!" they said. And they hid.

Trembling, Sir Garibald got off his motorbike and **crept into** the market place. Hot Nose could hardly bear to watch.

The second dragon was stamping its feet and breathing out fire.

In a high, trembling voice Sir Garibald called, "D...D...D...Dragon! G...Go away! Or I'll f...f...f...fight you!"

「就在那裡！」他們說著，然後全躲了起來。

加里波爵士顫抖地下車，緩緩走到市集裡頭。哈諾幾乎不敢看下去了。

那隻龍跺了跺腳，還一邊噴出火焰。

加里波爵士用發抖的聲音高聲說：「龍……龍……龍啊！走……走開，要不然我就要……對……對付你了！」

creep [krip] 動 緩慢地走
（過去式 crept [krεpt]）
creep into... 悄悄走進…

The dragon stood still and looked at him.

"Fight me! What for?"

"For f...f...frightening people," said Sir Garibald. "S...s...stamping your feet, and b...b...breathing out fire."

"How **misunderstood** can a dragon be?" **glared** the dragon. "Never **judge** a person till you know them! I'm not trying to frighten people. I'm cold. I'm trying to keep warm!"

龍動也不動地站在那兒看著他。

「對付我？為什麼？」

「因為……你用力跺腳，又噴……噴出火焰，嚇……壞了百姓。」加里波爵士說。

「你們怎麼可以這樣誤解我呢？」那隻龍瞪著眼睛生氣地說，「在還不了解別人時，絕不要妄下結論！我並不是要嚇人，我只是很冷，想要暖暖身子而已！」

misunderstand [ˌmɪsʌndɚˋstænd] 動 誤解
glare [glɛr] 動 怒目而視
judge [dʒʌdʒ] 動 評判

Sir Garibald looked **doubtfully** at the dragon. Was it telling the truth?

"In any case, I never eat people," added the dragon. "I'm a **vegetarian**. But I do feel the cold."

It blew out more fire, trying to warm its feet. Sir Garibald was sorry for it. He thought hard. Then he said, "Wait!"

He **unwound** the long woolly **scarf** he always wore when he rode his motorbike. Quickly he **wound** it round the dragon's neck.

加里波爵士懷疑地看著那隻龍，他說的可是真的嗎？

「不管怎樣，我是不會吃人的。」龍接著說。「我吃素。我不過是很怕冷而已。」

他又噴出更多的火來，想暖暖腳。加里波爵士同情地看著他，同時努力想著解決的辦法，然後說：「等一下！」

加里波爵士解開他騎車時圍著的長羊毛圍巾，很快地把圍巾繫在那隻龍的頸子上。

doubtfully [`daʊtfəlɪ] 副 懷疑地
vegetarian [ˌvɛdʒə`tɛrɪən] 名 素食主義者
unwind [ʌn`waɪnd] 動 解開
（過去式 unwound [ʌn`waʊnd]）
scarf [skɑrf] 名 圍巾
wind [waɪnd] 動 纏繞
（過去式 wound [waʊnd]）

Then he sat down and took off his shoes. He pulled off the warm **stretchy socks** he always wore when he rode his motorbike. He **fitted** his socks onto the dragon's back feet.

Next he reached into his pockets and pulled out the warm stretchy gloves he always had with him when he rode his motorbike. He **tugged** them onto the dragon's front feet.

"How's that?" he asked.

"Much better!" smiled the dragon.

然後他坐下來把鞋脫掉，再脫下他騎車時穿的保暖彈性襪，把襪子套在龍的後腳上。

接著，加里波爵士把手伸進口袋，拿出他騎車時戴的保暖彈性手套，用力地套進龍的前腳上。

「覺得如何？」他問。

「感覺好多了！」龍微笑著說。

stretchy [`strɛtʃɪ] 形 有彈性的
sock [sɑk] 名 短襪（通常用 socks）
fit [fɪt] 動 使適合
tug [tʌg] 動 用力拉

"Thank you. I can fly on now. I'm a long way from home, you know."

Sir Garibald stepped back. The dragon flapped its wings, rose into the air and flew off.

The villagers saw it go. They came running up.

"Well done!" they cried.

Hot Nose zoomed down.

"Aaaaah!" screamed the villagers.

「謝謝你，我現在可以飛行了。你知道，我已經離家很遠了。」

加里波爵士向後退了幾步，龍揮動翅膀，飛向天空，離開了。

村民看見龍離開，趕緊跑了出來。

「做得好耶！」他們大聲叫著。

哈諾也飛奔過來。

「啊！」村民尖叫著。

Then they remembered it was only Hot Nose.

Hot Nose was thinking about rewards...

The mayor of Nettleford stepped forward.

"Sir Knight, we should like you to have our reward after all," he said. "We *want* you to get electricity, and be able to play video games!"

然後才想起來那只是哈諾。

哈諾還在想著獎金……

尼陀福特村的村長走向前來。

「騎士大人，我們還是希望您收下獎金。這樣您才能接上電力，玩電腦益智遊戲。」他說。

"But —" **hesitated** Sir Garibald.

"Thank you!" cried Hot Nose, quickly accepting the money.

"You got rid of our dragon. We want to give you a reward **as well**!" cried the Greenways villagers. And they did.

「但是——」加里波爵士猶豫著。

「謝謝！」哈諾叫著，趕忙接下那些錢。

「您替我們除去了龍，我們同樣要給您獎金。」格林威治的村民喊著，也贈送了獎金。

hesitate [`hɛzə͵tet] 動 猶豫

as well　也

So Sir Garibald and Hot Nose had electricity put into the dark, creepy castle. It became a bright, uncreepy castle.

Sir Garibald had a great time, playing video games. He invited all the people (and especially the children) to come and play video games whenever they wanted to.

於是加里波爵士和哈諾為他們那座黑漆漆、陰森森的城堡接上了電，變成一座明亮、不再可怕的城堡。

加里波爵士玩著電腦益智遊戲，好不快活。他還邀請大家（尤其是小朋友）隨時到城堡來玩電腦益智遊戲。

Hot Nose invited them, as well. He had a plan. Every time he won a game — which would be often, because he would practice a lot — the loser would give him a **prize**....

哈諾當然也歡迎大家來玩。他有個計畫呢！他每贏得一場遊戲——這是很常發生的，因為他經常練習喲！——輸的人就要給他賞金……

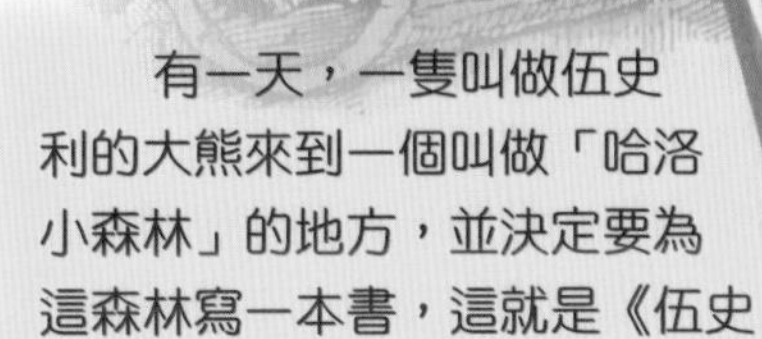

國家圖書館出版品預行編目資料

加里波爵士與噴火龍哈諾 = Sir Garibald and hot nose / Marjorie Newman 著；Christopher Masters 繪；刊欣媒體工作室譯
——初版. ——臺北市：三民，民88
面； 公分
ISBN 957-14-3000-5（平裝）

1.英國語言—讀本

805.18 88004005

網際網路位址 http://www.sanmin.com.tw

著作人 Marjorie Newman
繪圖者 Christopher Masters
譯　者 刊欣媒體工作室
發行人 劉振強
著作財產權人 三民書局股份有限公司
臺北市復興北路三八六號
發行所 三民書局股份有限公司
地址／臺北市復興北路三八六號
電話／二五〇〇六六〇〇
郵撥／〇〇〇九九九八——五號
印刷所 三民書局股份有限公司
門市部 復北店／臺北市復興北路三八六號
重南店／臺北市重慶南路一段六十一號
初　版 中華民國八十八年九月
編　號 S85481
定　價 新臺幣壹佰陸拾元整
行政院新聞局登記證局版臺業字第〇二〇〇號

ISBN 957-14-3000-5（平裝）

G